This book belongs to:

Luna Jepp radford Spanner

First published in 2020.
Sea School Stories, Staffordshire, England.

Text © 2020 Natalie Pritchard
Illustrations © 2020 Natalie Merheb

A CIP catalogue record for this book is available from the British Library.

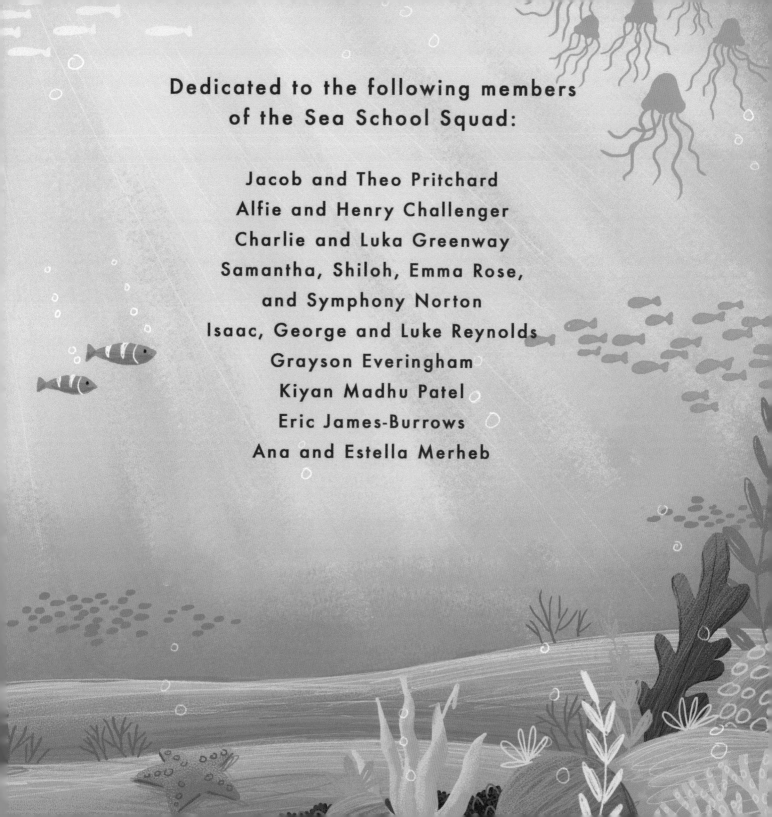

Dedicated to the following members
of the Sea School Squad:

Jacob and Theo Pritchard
Alfie and Henry Challenger
Charlie and Luka Greenway
Samantha, Shiloh, Emma Rose,
and Symphony Norton
Isaac, George and Luke Reynolds
Grayson Everingham
Kiyan Madhu Patel
Eric James-Burrows
Ana and Estella Merheb

DAISY the DOLPHIN
GETS INTO TROUBLE

NATALIE PRITCHARD   NATALIE MERHEB

Darting beneath the ENCHANTING blue seas,
Where seagulls were squabbling in a light ocean breeze,
DAISY THE DOLPHIN was doing her tricks,
Making some mischief with whistles and clicks.

When it was time to swim into her school,
Daisy did not want to follow the rule,
Throwing big tantrums and raising her voice,
Yes, Daisy quite often made a BAD CHOICE.

She dived into class so incredibly late,
Too busy chatting to notice Miss Eight.
"DAISY! The bell goes at quarter to nine!
Hurry, be quick and please get into line!"

Daisy got angry. Her face went bright red,
She shouted and pouted. Just guess what she said?
"STOP IT! I don't like being told what to do!
I really am NOT going to listen to you!"

Miss Eight had a quick, quiet word in her ear,
"No playtime for Daisy, just let me be clear."

Daisy felt sad as her classmates had fun,
She felt a bit sorry for what she had done.
She knew it was naughty, she knew it was wrong -
But could she stay out of trouble for long?

Next lesson was all about myths and old tales,
LEGENDS OF MERMAIDS as told by the whales.
With emerald green scales and long, golden hair,
Spotting a mermaid was a tricky affair.

So, pupils embarked on a thrilling school trek,
Down to the cave by the ancient shipwreck.
Miss Eight whispered:
"**Shhh**, please do not make a sound,
Mermaids are shy –
they don't like to be found."

All of the pupils remained calm and still,
Keeping so silent took patience and skill.
A GLIMMER OF GOLD soon
peeked out from the rocks,
Was it a MERMAID
with long, golden locks?

Then...Daisy let out an almighty big SCREECH!
A screeching so LOUD it was heard on the beach!
OH NO!

The glimmer was gone just as quick as a flash,
All that was left was a ripple - a SPLASH!

Hopes of them finding a mermaid that day,
Were dashed, thanks to Daisy. So, what did she say?
"Quiet is boring and silence is dull,
So I let out a SCREECH sound, just like a seagull!"

But when Daisy's friends really started to cry,
Daisy felt guilty and sighed a big sigh.
She knew it was naughty, she knew it was wrong -
But could she stay out of trouble for long?

In Maths class, the pupils were counting CLAM PEARLS,

There were plenty
for all of the boys and the girls.

Counting in twos and then taking away,
Sharing clam pearls was a GREAT GAME TO PLAY.

Daisy instructed: "I simply won't share!"
She snatched all the pearls and she didn't play fair.
Then **CRACK!** went the clams as they smacked to the floor,
The pearls all spilled out and were washed to the shore.

CRACK!!!!!

Miss Eight cried, "OH, DAISY, it's such a great shame.
But now you're not trusted with playing the game."
She knew it was naughty, she knew it was wrong,
But could she stay out of trouble for long?

Next was a trip to the huge plastic pile,
MOUNTAINS OF RUBBISH just stretching for miles.
Miss Eight wished to make all her pupils aware,
Of mess MADE BY HUMANS, who don't really care.

Big plastic bags, crumpled bottles and waste,
Spoiling the ocean; discarded in haste.

Miss Eight said: "Stay close and do not touch a thing.

DAISY! Please move from that old plastic ring."

Daisy then chose not to take the advice,
She nudged the old ring and she tugged on it twice.
OOOPS! It came loose and then caught on her beak,
She pulled and she panicked and started to SHRIEK!
Then....

The **GINORMOUS** pile came tumbling down fast,
Down on to Daisy! Her friends watched and gasped!
Try as she might, Daisy couldn't get free,
LISTENING WAS CRUCIAL, she started to see.

CRASH!!!!!

PULLLLLLLLLLLLLLLLLLLLLL!

Miss Eight tried to help, but poor DAISY WAS STUCK,
Tangled in plastic, she'd ran out of luck.

Time rolled on by; the moon danced on the tide,
They couldn't free Daisy, and oh how SHE CRIED!
Just as they thought that she couldn't be saved,
TOM TURTLE appeared, on the crest of a wave.

Tom was an oldie - he knew lots of things,
But could he help Daisy escape from the ring?
He told Daisy how she should twist her big tail,
"DO AS I SAY," he said. "Or you will fail."

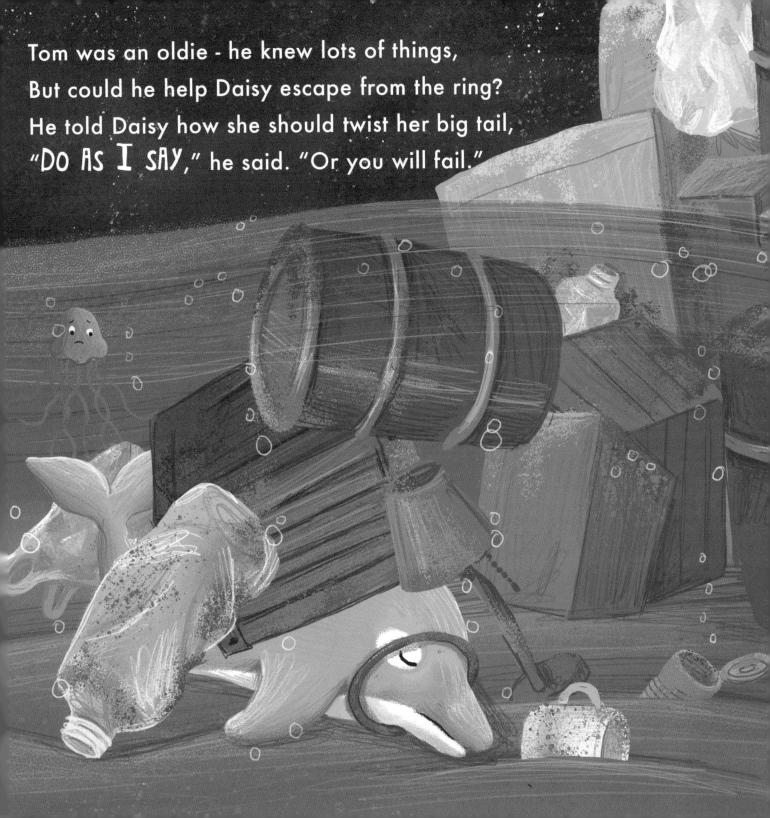

"Twist to the left and turn once to the right.
Then wriggle and jiggle with all your strong might!"

Daisy now listened and did what Tom asked,
OOOOOOFFFF! It came loose! She was free at long last!

She thanked the kind turtle, who went on his way,
Before he swam off, he had something to say:
"Life is about all the choices we make,
FOLLOW advice. CHOOSE the right path to take."

She knew it was naughty, she knew it was wrong -
So, she made the right choice from that day on!
Daisy remembered to stick to the rules
To take a deep breath, and then
STOP, THINK, and CHOOSE.

FACTS ABOUT DOLPHINS

Did you know.....?

• Dolphins are extremely intelligent mammals who communicate with each other through different whistle and click sounds. They each have their own signature whistle or 'name'.

• They can jump as high as 6 metres out of the water and can swim up to speeds of 30mph – as fast as a car!

• They are carnivores and love to eat small fishes and squid.

• There are over 30 different species of dolphin and they are found in waters all over the world.

• A baby dolphin is known as a calf and they stay with their mother for up to eight years.

• Dolphins are very social and playful. They live in groups, known as pods, which hunt together and look after each other when they are sick. The pods can have 1,000 members or more!

• Pollution, fishing and hunting remain the biggest threats to dolphins. Sadly, each year over 100,000 marine mammals are killed by either being tangled in plastic or eating small plastic particles.

SEA SCHOOL STORIES

· ENCOURAGING EMOTIONAL INTELLIGENCE ·

Daisy the Dolphin is part of the Sea School Stories series. The books aim to support children's social and emotional learning through magical ocean adventures

FREE RESOURCES AND TEACHER PLANNING AVAILABLE AT

www.seaschoolstories.co.uk

FOLLOW SEA SCHOOL STORIES:

facebook.com/groups/seaschoolstories
instagram @seaschoolstories

Printed in Great Britain
by Amazon